I LIKE

MALAMUTES!

Linda Bozzo

AMERICAN CANINE ASSOCIATION INC.

ACA

America's Largest Veterinary
Health Tracking Canine
Registry

OFFICIAL SEAL ®

It is the mission of the American Canine Association (ACA) to provide registered dog owners with the educational support needed for raising, training, showing, and breeding the healthiest pets expected by responsible pet owners throughout the world. Through our activities and services, we encourage and support the dog world in order to promote best-known husbandry standards as well as to ensure that the voice and needs of our customers are quickly and properly addressed.

Our continued support, commitment, and direction are guided by our customers, including veterinary, legal, and legislative advisors. ACA aims to provide the most efficient, cooperative, and courteous service to our customers and strives to set the standard for education and problem solving for all who depend on our services.

For more information, please visit www.acacanines.com, email customerservice@acadogs.com, phone 1-800-651-8332, or write to the American Canine Association at PO Box 121107, Clermont, FL 34712.

Published in 2019 by Enslow Publishing, LLC.
101 W. 23rd Street, Suite 240, New York, NY 10011

Library of Congress Cataloging-in-Publication Data

Names: Bozzo, Linda, author.
Title: I like Malamutes! / Linda Bozzo.
Description: New York, NY : Enslow Publishing, 2019. | Series: Discover dogs with the American Canine Association | Includes bibliographical references and index. | Audience: Grades K to 3.
Identifiers: LCCN 2017045146| ISBN 9780766096677 (library bound) | ISBN 9780766096684 (pbk.) | ISBN 9780766096691 (6 pack)
Subjects: LCSH: Alaskan Malamute—Juvenile literature.
Classification: LCC SF429.A67 B69 2017 | DDC 636.73—dc23
LC record available at https://lccn.loc.gov/2017045146

Printed in the United States of America

To Our Readers: We have done our best to make sure all websites in this book were active and appropriate when we went to press. However, the author and the publisher have no control over and assume no liability for the material available on those websites or on any websites they may link to. Any comments or suggestions can be sent by email to customerservice@enslow.com.

Photo Credits: Cover, p. 1 Eric Isselee/Shutterstock.com; p. 3 (left) Serhii Yushkov/Shutterstock.com; p. 3 (right) otsphoto/Shutterstock.com; p. 5 Pete Leonard/Corbis/Getty Images; p. 6 Zuzule/Shutterstock.com; p. 9 Grisha Bruev/Shutterstock.com; p. 10 ArtMarie/Vetta/Getty Images; pp. 13, 17 Yuriy Koronovskiy/Shutterstock.com; p. 13 (collar) graphicphoto/iStock/Thinkstock, (bed) Luisa Leal Photography/Shutterstock.com, (brush) In-Finity/Shutterstock.com, (food and water bowls) exopixel/Shutterstock.com, (leash, toys) © iStockphoto.com/Liliboas; p. 14 Sushitsky Sergey/Shutterstock.com; 18 Evdoha_spb/Shutterstock.com; p. 19 Vasyl Syniuk/Shutterstock.com; p. 21 Olga Kuzyk/Shutterstock.com.

Enslow Publishing
101 W. 23rd Street
Suite 240
New York, NY 10011
USA
enslow.com

CONTENTS

IS A MALAMUTE RIGHT FOR YOU?

Malamutes need lots of exercise. If you are part of an active family, a malamute could be right for you.

The malamute is the largest and one of the oldest Arctic sled dogs.

A DOG OR A PUPPY?

Malamutes are smart, but these puppies can be hard to train. If you do not have time to train a puppy, you may want an older malamute instead.

This breed is best for an experienced dog owner.

LOVING YOUR MALAMUTE

Show your malamute love by taking him to play in the snow! Malamutes love cold weather. These dogs also love their families and will want to spend time with you.

The name "malamute" comes from the Mahlemut people of Alaska who bred these dogs.

EXERCISE

Malamutes need long walks on a leash. This breed would rather be camping and hiking than playing games like fetch.

Bred as sled dogs, malamutes are strong and love to pull things.

FEEDING YOUR MALAMUTE

Malamutes can be fed wet or dry dog food. Ask a veterinarian (vet), a doctor for animals, which food is best for your dog and how much to feed her.

Give your malamute fresh, clean water every day.

Remember to keep your dog's food and water dishes clean. Dirty dishes can make a dog sick.

Do not feed your dog people food. It can make her sick.

Your new dog will need:

a collar with a tag

a bed

a brush

food and water dishes

a leash

toys

Malamutes have a beautiful waterproof double coat.

GROOMING

Malamutes shed, especially in the spring and fall. This means their hair falls out. Your malamute will need to be brushed and combed often.

A malamute's thick nails will need to be clipped. A vet or groomer can show you how. Your dog's ears should be cleaned, and his teeth should be brushed by an adult.

WHAT YOU SHOULD KNOW

Without enough exercise, malamutes can get into trouble. They may bark or dig.

Most malamutes don't like cats or other small animals.

A home with lots of space to run and walk is best for this large dog.

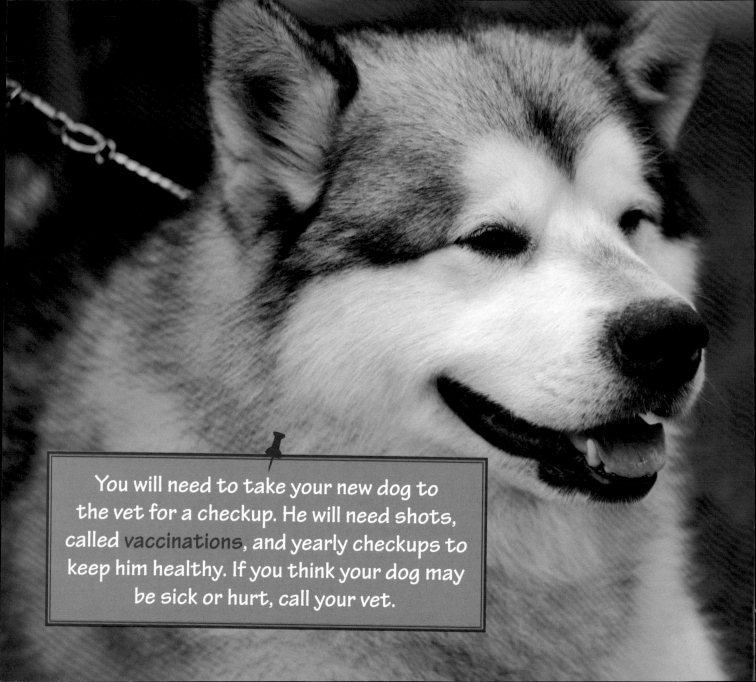

You will need to take your new dog to the vet for a checkup. He will need shots, called vaccinations, and yearly checkups to keep him healthy. If you think your dog may be sick or hurt, call your vet.

A GOOD FRIEND

Your malamute will be your friend for a long time. She will enjoy lots of family outings to the park.

Malamutes live around 10 to 15 years.

NOTE TO PARENTS

It is important to consider having your dog spayed or neutered when the dog is young. Spaying and neutering are operations that prevent unwanted puppies and can help improve the overall health of your dog.

It is also a good idea to microchip your dog, in case he or she gets lost. A vet will implant a microchip under the skin containing an identification number that can be scanned at a vet's office or animal shelter. The microchip registry is contacted, and the company uses the ID number to look up your information from a database.

Some towns require licenses for dogs, so be sure to check with your town clerk.

For more information, speak with a vet.

There are many dogs, young and old, waiting to be adopted from animal shelters and rescue groups.

active Always keeping busy.

fetch To go after a toy and bring it back.

groomer A person who bathes and brushes dogs.

leash A chain or strap that attaches to a dog's collar.

shed When dog hair falls out so new hair can grow.

vaccinations Shots that dogs need to stay healthy.

veterinarian (vet) A doctor for animals.

waterproof Not able to get wet.

Books

Markovics, Joyce. *Sled Dogs*. New York, NY: Bearport Publishing, 2014.

Morey, Allan. *Sled Dogs on the Job*. Mankato, MN: The Child's World, 2017.

Petrie, Kristin. *Alaskan Malamutes*. Minneapolis, MN: Abdo Publishing, 2014.

Websites

American Canine Association Inc., Kids Corner
www.acakids.com
Visit the official website of the American Canine Association.

National Geographic for Kids, Pet Central
kids.nationalgeographic.com/explore/pet-central
Learn more about dogs and other pets at the official site of the National Geographic Society for Kids.

INDEX